Rhythms of My Heart

Erotic Tales

Quishauna Hairston

ISBN: 9798677645914

Before diving into this book, I must start by saying that this is for people with an open mind only… If you are homophobic, this is not the book for you…If you are not truly open to sexuality, this is not the book for you…If you don't have a good imagination, this is not the book for you…If you get offended easily, this is not the book for you... If you still haven't faced the reality of the world we live in, this is not the book for you…If you have a fixed mindset, this is not the book for you…

This book is extremely raunchy…From poetry to short

stories and back again…This is for entertainment only…This book is true to the thoughts that are in my head at the current moment of writing each and every poem…This book is intended to resonate with individuals that have sexual fantasies they may be afraid to explore in the natural... This is a safe place for people to live out fantasies through their imagination… With that being said… Let the Games begin…

I hope that you enjoy it.

Titles

Wet

Cum Inside

Joy Ride

Once Again

Back

Stranger Things

Good Boy

3 O'clock Blues

If I was a Boy

Pick Up Line

Never Ending Story

It's Love

Wet

I can feel a rush of my natural juices…
Glide down my inner thigh…

As I admire the dirt in his fingernails…

You see most women enjoy a well-groomed man…

But it's the working man for me…

As he hands me my paperwork to sign...

I can see a vein throbbing in his neck…

My mind went ballistic…

As I imaged that same vein pulsating from down below…

I grab my keys and make my way for the door…

As I can hear the gusting of my guilty pleasures ready for more…

Cum Inside

Knock…

Knock…

Knock…

I've been anticipating this moment…

The moment the maintenance man would come knocking at my door…

Come inside…

I said…

He makes his way to my kitchen sink to unclog the pipes…

Wishing he was draining me instead…

I leaned back against the counter…

So I could get a good view of him…

While he laid back halfway under the sink…

From the dip in his top lip…

To the size of his feet…

Every inch of him was turning me on…

I began to admire his print bulging in his dickie pants…

I took a glance up at his face…

Now knowing what caused his arousal…

His eyes were engaged with my hard nipples…

That were greeting him through my white T'shirt…

Got'em…

I thought to myself…

Cause I knew exactly what I was doing when I put it on…

I asked him if I could help him with anything…

He studder…

Not knowing what to say…

I didn't need for him to say anything any damn way…

I knew what I wanted…

And I was determined to get it…

His eyes still on me…

I began to rub my breast…

I could feel my puss begin to tickle…

As the trickles of my essence began to leak…

I slowly walked over…

Straddled him just enough for him to explore with his eyes…

What was under my skirt…

He moved his hand to grab my left ankle…

Started to make his way up my leg…

AHT…

AHT…

AHT…

No touching…

And he obeyed…

I dropped down to sit on his hard rock…

As I unbuckled his pants…

I took him in my right hand with a firm grip…

Stroking up and down…

While rotating my wrist in a counterclockwise motion…

His head dropped back….

Gasping with each stroke…

Still stroking with my right…

While using my left hand to lift my left breast into my mouth…

The tickle between my legs getting more intense…

I could feel a puddle of my essence fill up on his lap…

One stroke…

Two strokes…

Three strokes…

Four!!!!...

We had an explosion together…

My hands are gifted…

I knew right when he was ready…

And I wanted to share the moment of climax with him…

He laid there in disbelief…

As I stood up…

Then proceeded to make my way to the rest room to grab a towel…

I asked him to remove his pants…

He started to yank them off quickly…

Slow down baby…

I calmly said to him…

I only needed them off of him…

But not to fuck…

They needed to be washed and dried by the time he finished up working…

Him still looking at me completely puzzled…

I just had to go ahead and tell him…

Thanks for the favor…

He got me a little warmed up for my husband for when he returned home…

By the expression on his face…

I could tell that he felt used…

But fuck it…

He just had a moment that he will never forget…

Damn I'm such a tease…

Joy Ride

It's been a long a day…

I can't wait another second to get to my man…

All I could think of is how the sun beams on his olive skin…

He walks out the double doors of his office building…

With a surprised look upon his face…

I knew he wasn't expecting to see me…

Being that we had a minor disagreement this morning…

I wasn't one to hold grudges like he do…

It was time to make up…

I was resting my soft ass against the hood of his car…

When he approached…

Rocking a fitted red trench coat…

And all black leather thigh high boots…

He didn't say a word…

He just walked over to the passenger side…

And opened the car door for me…

I stood straight up…

Twisting my hips with every step…

As I made my way over…

Stepped right up in his face to lick his lips with the tip of my tongue…

Slowly prying them open to twirl my tongue around his…

I took a step back…

Looked at my man…

And smirked…

I could see the heavens in his eyes…

As he looked me up and down…

He told me to get in…

I listened…

He closed the door…

Then sprinted his way to the driver side to get in himself…

As soon as he was seated…

I leaned over to kiss him behind his ear…

Then took my togue to lick down his neck…

Sealed with a juicy kiss…

As he shifted the car into drive…

My hand made its way down to feel his excitement…

I caressed him gently…

As he drove…

I began to unbutton his pants…

Then sat back to take off my coat…

He used one hand to steer and the other to unzip his pants...

I grabbed the steering wheel to guide the car…

As he leaned up to pull his pants down enough for me to do what I do best…

Him now back in control of the wheel…

I took my breast into my hands…

Push them together to get a good grip around his dick…

Gracing its head with a kiss from my lips…

Before wrapping my tongue around it…

Up and down…

Up and down…

Up and down…

My head and breast bop…

Up and down…

Up and down…

Up and down…

I take a moment to breathe…

Look up at him just to make sure his eye were still on the road…

They were…

But his grip on the steering wheel was stern...

I laughed and said…

You gone hurt yourself…

Then dived back in for more…

I could feel the tears rolling down my face…

As I took him deeper and deeper into my mouth…

By the movement of his body…

I could tell that he had just clinched his hind cheeks…

He was ready to shed his load…

Up and down…

Faster and faster…

Ready to receive every drop of him…

Ummmmm…

The sweet taste of his love darts to the back of my throat…

I take a deep swallow to keep from chocking on a single drop…

I picked my head up…

Looked him in the face…

To check to see if he was still mad…

I can tell that he wasn't…

But he was a good man…

He deserved what I had for him next…

Mouth still moist from all his loving…

I kissed him gently on his cheek…

Then angled the head good enough for him to still see the road…

While I kissed his lips…

I gave him a moment to breathe…

Removing my boots…

There was nothing left to get in our way…

Being that I was already naked…

Because I had nothing on under my coat…

I turn around to face the seat…

Lifted my right leg over him…

Then proceeded the shift my body to the right…

To position myself perfectly on top of him..

Took my left hand to grip his already hard dick…

Holding it steady…

I eased my way down the slippery slope…

Instant gushing…

Like stirring a pot of macaroni…

Tasting him always got me aroused…

More than any four play could…

I could feel his dick filling up my walls…

It always feels so good to have my tight grip around him…

I slithered my body like I snake…

As I pounce up and down…

Mouth wide open trying try to catch my breath…

Between each deep breath I took in each moment of fulfillment…

All I could hear from him was passionate grunts…

Between whispers of I love You…

Red light…

Green light…

We were on go…

As we are now cruising the boulevard…

Almost home…

Though I'm not done with him yet…

I placed each foot on each side of his seat…

Pushed the auto bottom on side…

To lean back the seat just a little…

Enough for him to still be able to see…

Enough to stop my ass from honking the horn…

Squat after Squat…

I bounce on him…

Using every muscle in my thighs that I could…

Feeling the tip of him…

Beating up my stomach from the inside…

We approach our home…

He eases the car into the garage…

Trying to hold the wheel steady…

To prevent from hitting my car…

The garage door begins to close…

With every second of the door easing down…

Our love making got more intense…

He wraps his arms around my back…

Pulling himself into me closely…
Taking the nipple of both of my breast into his mouth…

He knows what I like…

Definitely knows what will take me there…

My body begins to tremble…

I collapse limp in his arms…

He grabs my hips…

Then proceeds to thrust upward…

Kissing my neck…

To biting harder and harder…

His right leg began to shake…

He screams out with a roar of excitement…

He looked at me…

As I looked him in his eyes..

What a joy ride…

Once Again

We said we were over…

But do things really come to an end?...

It's been a minute since we've even spoken…

But my body is craving his love…

I was laying in bed…

Had just about rubbed my clit to death with my bullet…

But it was time for the real thing…

A new pleasure partner just wasn't the answer either…

As bad as I needed to be fulfilled…

There was no way I was taking that chance and wasting my time…

I pulled out my phone and began to caress my clit once again…

This time only using my finger…

I pressed record…

Started recording this thrill that I was giving myself…

Then pressed send…

He responded immediately with a…

I'm on my way…

As if I he was sitting by the phone…

Anticipating my call…

I finished myself off…

As I was waiting for his arrival…

No way I wasn't going to finish enjoying the pleasure I was already giving to myself…

I could feel a stream of shock moved through my body…

Just in time to catch the knock at the door…

I made my way to the door…

Ass naked…

Juices dripping on the floor with every step…

Was no need to cover up just for him to have to take it right off…

I opened the door…

He rushed me…
Scooping my body off the floor…

The heavy door slammed itself closed…

As he carried me down the hall…

Kissing me passionately....

I'm guessing he was too thirsty for me…

Being that he didn't even make it to the bedroom…

He stopped in his tracks in the kitchen…

Sat me up on the kitchen island…

Looked me in my eyes…

Saying…

Baby I miss you…

I wanted to say duh…

But instead…

I just smiled…

As he kneeled…

Meeting my right foot with his mouth…

Beginning to twirl his tongue between each toe…

Of course to be fair…

He does the same with my left…

Left foot still in his mouth…

He stands…

Then rested my leg on his shoulder…

He began to bury his face deep in my juices…

Sucking up every drop that was already there…

Just for me to rain all over his face…

Again…

And again…

And again…

I had so many orgasms at this point…

I know my girl was swollen…

But with the pleasure he was bringing me…

Aint no way I wasn't going to let him go further…

He stood up…

Beard oiled down with the thrill of me…

He leaned in for me to taste myself…
As he made his way inside me…

Hard thrusting…

Ass sliding back and forth…

As he goes in and out…

I grip his back with my nails…

Scratching him up with each thrust…

I lean back as he grabbed my neck…

Squeezing it tighter each time he glides himself deeper and deeper…

My eyes rolled back in my head as he still chokes me…

Then meets my lady with his face again…

He could tell I was almost there…

By the way I began to grip the back of his head…

He quickly stood up…

Bombarded his way back inside me…

Just in time to feel my wall contractions…

Gripping on him even tighter…

His pulse now beating at the same steady beat of each contraction…

He lays his head on my stomach…

For the once more…

Or shall I say until the next time…

Back

I watched her the entire night…

Patiently waiting on the party to be over…

My girls were drunk…

Due to ladies' night being a success…

It has been a moment since I saw her…

Last time was fun…

But this time I wanted it from the back…

Everyone made themselves comfy…

She stayed alert because she knew what was up…

Without me even having to say a word…

After everyone was out…

She made her way over to me…

I lifted her dress above head to remove it…

I laid her on her back…

Then slid her panties off with my teeth..

It was on…

Diving in headfirst…

This wasn't no love thing…

So I would never confuse it by kissing…

She always tasted so good…

Always so fresh…

Most importantly always ready for whatever…

I used my tongue in one way…

While using my fingers to massage her inner G spot…

A puddle filled up the cuff of my hand…

As her sensual goods flowed from within her…

As I'm going…

I take my free hand to lift her bottom up…

I removed my fingers from inside her for a moment…

As I began to lick my way down…

My Tongue now meeting the crack of her ass…

As I flipped her over to her stomach…

She arched her back…

As a lick every inch from one end to the next…

Once she was good and dripping…

I parted her ass wide open so I could ease my clit in to meet hers…

They rub together intensely…

Each getting wetter and wetter…

Clits getting more and more sensitive in excitement…

I could feel her running down her legs…

As I ran down mine…

I entered her again with two fingers…

Then proceeding to put my thumb from the same hand in her glory hole…

Grabbed her fat ass with my free hand…

Using it to keep my balance…

As my fingers pumped in and out of her…

I just wanted to feel her nut once more…

Being a pleaser is what pleased me…

Now I'm just patiently waiting for the next time…

I can get it from the back…

Stranger Things

This guy has been asking me out for a while…

And my radar is always on point…

I could tell that he is into stranger things…

As I tell my girls..

Don't let them looks fool you…

Every man is up for debate…

He was definitely a good look…

If tall, dark, and handsome was a person…

It would for certain be him…

He sat across the dinner table from me…

Conversation interesting …

But I became bored with that…

I wanted to get to the meat and potatoes…

Or shall I say…

Stranger things…

I knew his background…

And like most men…

If they did the unspeakable…

They would deny it to the death of them…

But I wasn't going for that…

I proceeded to dig deep…

Because later…

Once it was all said and done…

I was going to dig deep…

Conversation led from one thing to the other…

I had him right where I wanted him…

Submissive he was indeed…

And I was about to enjoy him…

Enjoy him in the way he truly desired…

We made our way to his place…

The drinks and shots had finally kicked in…

I made myself at home once we enter…

Ask him to guide to me to the washroom...

I began to undress as I turned on the shower…

We both entered…

I washed him from top to bottom…

Then he returned the favor…

We made our way for his room…

I say…

Show me your stranger things…

He reaches in the top of his closet…

Pull out a lock box…

Then proceed to unlock it…

To my surprise…

He had more than what I even bargained for…

But fuck it…

There was no turning back…

Cause I was into stranger things…

I reached in to grab two pairs of handcuffs…

Cuffed him…

Faced down…

Each wrist secured to the bed…

I strap myself up tight…

Now it was time to dig deep…

A quarter worth of lube…

That should do the trick…

As it eased from the tube upon the area some consider an exit only…

He quivered with joy…

Intrigued by what was next…

One inch…

Two inch…

Three inch …

Four inch…

Five Inch…

With each inch…

He screamed out more…

Six inch…

Seven inch…

Eight inch…

Screams for more…

Nine inch…

Ten inch..

Eleven inch…

More…

Twelve inches deep…

Still begging for more…

He gains more moisture from himself…

Cream showering every inch…

As I go deeper and deeper..

He's begging for more…

Each time turning me on more…

Sexy and submissive….

Just the way I like them…

What we do is what we do…

No one will ever know…

As the feel my knee getting weak…

I think its time to finish him off…

I had him to bend his knees…

Enough to lift his ass to sit in my lap…

I reach around to hold him from the front…

I stroke him from the front and the back …

At the same time…

He bites the pillow…

As he presses his face in it…

As he enjoys the final moments of stranger things…

Good Boy

He had been a good boy…

And good boys are celebrated…

It was a random day…

Cause I aint the type of bitch that only gives gifts on birthdays…

I had planned an entire weekend for us…

I cabin get away…

But he knew I was always full of surprises…

We arrived…

But it was late…

So I said we would settle in…

Enjoy a relaxing moment in the hot tub…

Allow the night to take us to places we never been…

While he prepared himself…

I unlocked the door for our special guest…

Champagne on ice…

He now joins me in the hot tub…

A toast to us…

A toast for infinite love…

Followed by a toast to good times…

I had his full attention…

So he didn't notice the curvy women approaching us…

I place my hands on his shoulders…

As I slide him back against the side of the jacuzzi…

She the placed her hands on his shoulders…

As I removed mine…

He jumped in shock…

Looked behind himself…

Then began to gaze upon his surprise…

Relax…

I told him…

He turned back to me…

And did just that…

As she rubbed his shoulders…

She leaned down to plant a kiss on my lips…

He knew I had a woman…

I loved them both…

But I loved them separately…

He's been a good boy...

So for once I would let him enjoy the both of us…

I stepped out…

Grabbed his hand to lead him out…

Dabbed him off…

Then led him to the massage table waiting on him…

We started with a massage…

She took care of the top…

While I handled the bottom…

As he laid on his stomach…

I enjoyed watching him

explore her body with his hands…

I whispered to him…

It's time to flip over baby…

Our hand rubbed his body…

Hands meeting in the middle as she climbs upon his face…

While my face was looking eyes to eye…

Making that single eye disappear in my mouth…

As she explored his face with her yoni…

His nose inhaling the fresh scent of her tight ass…

He used his to grab her thighs…

Pulling her into his face…

He aint want no room for air…

Him rock hard…

Licking up and down his bulging vain…

Before taking him in to meet my tonsils…

They both scream out…

As she exploded on his face…

And he releases in my mouth…

We let him up…

Two steps ahead of him…

She bends over the massage table…

He lifts me up…

Places me on her back…

He enters her…

As his face meets my happy place…

Stroking with each flick of his tongue…

My love runs down into hers…

Making his entry to her even more desirable…

I burst in celebration…

Knowing that my good boy was enjoying himself...

As we begin to switch positions…

I decided to sit this one out…

I sit back and watch my loves enjoy the love I get from each of them…

3 O'clock Blues

I got those 3 o'clock blues…

Too early to get off work…

But too deep in my day to leave early…

It has been a minute since I had a fix…

And my body was craving a tune up…

Ugh….

I got these 3 o'clock blues…

All I can do is imagine his body rubbing against mine…

Sweat dripping from nose…

Gliding down the center of my dirty pillows...

These damn 3 o'clock blues…

Got me rocking my legs side to side….

Wishing I was feeling something real between my thighs…

Fuck these 3 o'clock blues…

I can't take it anymore…

Just a little touch wont hurt…

Hell it's just me…

No one will see…

Letting go of these 3 o'clock blues…

As I glide my fingers like the clock on the wall…

Exploring myself gentle and slow…

Giving myself what I need to get through the day…

What 3'oclock blues…

When I closed my eyes…

And fantasied about what I was missing…

3 o'clock became 3:15…

3:15 became 3:30…

As I kept myself cumin…

For each time I came I only wanted more…

3 o'clock to 4 o'clock…

I was getting out of control…

But I couldn't stop my hand from doing me a good deed…

Hand giving me everything I need…

4'oclock to 4:15…

Sending each call to voicemail…

4:15 to 4:30…

Another round with myself…

Til I heard a sound…

Opened my eye to catch my boss pleasing himself…

I was so engaged in me…

I didn't hear him walk in…

4:30 to 4:45…

We lock eyes as we both continued our mutual masturbation…
5'clock strikes…

We were both relieved of our 3 o'clock blues…

If I Was a Boy

God knew not to make me a boy…

Because if I was a boy…

I would tell everyone I crossed paths with to suck my dick…

Men and Women…

Running trains on all kinds of things…

Big…

Small…

Thick…

Skinny…

Short…

Tall…

I wouldn’t discriminate…

I would fuck them all…

Bend’em…

Slip’em…

Cum up in ‘em…

I would be like a Dog…

Dick for anything I can put in own…

If I was a boy…

I’d probably be a porn star…

Maybe transgender…

So I could suck my titties…

And be flexible enough to lick my own balls…

If I was a boy…

I’d have long hair…

So I can have a shorty braid it down…

As I talk her out her underwear…

If I was a boy…

I would be a lot of things…

Man by day…

Do drag at night…

Befriend the baddest bitches…

Just to have their legs up all night…

If I was a boy…

I would be some old lady's boy toy…

Tell her all the things she loves to hear...

Give it to her right…

For the right price...

If I was boy…

I simply wouldn't be no good…

Wrap it up?...

No way…

I want to feel it all…

All day…

If only I was a boy…

Pickup Line

I don't have no pickup lines…
I only tell the truth…
Smile and grin…
As I watch you get loose…
I don't have no pickup line…
I only tell the truth…
Listening to you laugh…
When I say I wont call you tomorrow…
Cause you think I'm just joshing…
I don't have no pickup line…
I only tell the truth…

Telling you I love you…

Cause I do…

But that don't mean I want more than just a good time from you…

I don't have no pickup line…

I only tell the truth…

I called you up because I said I wanted talk…

Talk about you putting your face in my lap that is…

I don't have no pickup line…

I only tell the truth…

I wasn't smiling when I asked you to get up and leave…

You gave it up…

Now it's time raise up…

I don’t have no pickup line…

I only tell the truth…

Not once did I ever mention an us…

So stop asking what we going to do…

I don’t have no pickup line…

I only tell the truth…

It’s been fun…

Not it’s time for me to run…

Cause you tried to hit me with your pickup line…

Now it’s done back fired on you…

Never Ending Story

Each day of my life is the same…

I go out to sleep with someone else…

Just to enjoy the encounters with my husband…

It's something about him unknowingly sucking another man cum from my pussy...

Or maybe how tight it is after another man has swelled me up…

Man is he a fool…

Though I love him…

My addiction is my never-ending story…

An addiction that keeps me stepping away for more…

Maybe it's the kisses he gives me…

After another man shaft has been in my mouth…

He says he loves the way my lips taste…

When really, he is tasting him, him, and him…

My addition is a never-ending story...

Especially since he loves the taste…

But the gag is…

I didn't know my husband follows me every day…

After I make my rounds…

He’s making his…

Tasting me off him, him, and him…

Coming home just to taste more of them…

The cycle just repeats…

In our never-ending story…

Its Love

It's been a long time since I've saw you…

But as you walked in…

All our memories came back to me…

Conversation led to…

I kiss you here…

You kiss me there…

But this aint going nowhere…

Because I can't let you back in…

You pull me in tight as you stroke yourself…

With only minutes to spare…

You kiss me harder…

As you stroke harder…

Your lips rest against mine…

As you have reached your climax…

You look me in my eyes…

Followed by the word…

Damn…

As you gazed upon me as if I was the devil…

No penetration…

But the orgasmic feeling was just intense…

It was like saying hello again…

After saying final goodbyes…

Left me asking myself…

Why this feeling again...

For this is real love…

Something that we both share…

But I say goodbye to you again…

Even though it's love…

If you made it to the end, THANK YOU FOR READING…. Please leave review with your honest feedback.

www.ingramcontent.com/pod-product-compliance
Lightning Source LLC
LaVergne TN
LVHW091038150826
845672LV00006BA/1871

* 9 7 9 8 6 7 7 6 4 5 9 1 4 *